POCKET

I0534998

Pour Lucie Françoise Julié

Methuen/Moonlight
First published 1981 by William Heinemann Ltd
Copyright © 1980 by Colin McNaughton
First published 1983 in Pocket Bears by
Methuen Children's Books Ltd, 11 New Fetter
Lane, London EC4 in association with
Moonlight Publishing Ltd, 131 Kensington
Church Street, London W8

Printed in Italy by La Editoriale Libraria

ISBN 0 907144 34 9

KING NONN THE WISER

written and illustrated by
Colin McNaughton

methuen ☽ moonlight

Many years ago, in a land north of
Nonse and just to the right of
Rong, lived a king called Nonn the
Wiser. He was a peaceful fellow who
liked nothing better than to be left alone
with his books. But his people grew
restless, and one day the Prime Minister
decided he must speak to the King.

With his talking raven perched on his
shoulder, the Prime Minister climbed the
winding staircase to King Nonn's study.

"Your Majesty," said the Prime Minister, "something must be done. Your people are angry. They don't like the way you sit up here reading all day. They want a king who can fight dragons and slay giants, like King Blagard of Rong. You must go on an adventure and show them you are a king they can be proud of."

"Oh dear," said the King. "I'm far

too short-sighted to slay dragons, and I wouldn't even know where to start looking for a giant. Oh bother, Prime Minister, what's a king to do?''

''Your father, King Nonn the Less, left an old map that will tell you where to go,'' said the Prime Minister. ''You will find all you need in the armoury. But you must hurry, Your Majesty—your subjects are impatient.''

King Nonn put down his book
with a sigh. He never liked going to
the armoury. It was full of weapons
King Nonn the Less had used, and the
dust made him sneeze. But he
unlocked the door and poked about
until, at the bottom of a trunk, he
found the map.

"This must be the one," said King Nonn to himself. "Giants, dragons, witches—even damsels in distress. I'm bound to have an adventure if I follow this. Now, what else do I need?"

Feeling more cheerful, King Nonn picked up a sword and a lance and went to saddle his horse Palfrey.

While King Nonn was preparing
himself for the journey the Prime
Minister was up on the balcony with
his raven.

"Fly away, Raven," said the Prime
Minister. "Follow the King and keep
an eye on him. If he gets into trouble,
fly back and tell me so I can send
help. We don't want His Majesty
hurt."

King Nonn's
subjects lined the
castle walls and cheered as the King
rode out on his horse. He turned to
wave farewell.

"I expect that's the last time I'll
ever see my beautiful castle," he said
gloomily to Palfrey.

And so King Nonn set forth on his
great adventure. He rode till he came
in sight of the Land of Giants; and as
he rode, he talked to his horse Palfrey.
This is what he said.

"Well, Palfrey, old friend, this must be the Land of Giants. Can't see any, though. I'll try shouting. Come out and fight, you cowardly oafs! Come out and fight! Oh, I do feel a fool, stumbling about shouting at giants. Ah well, let's press on."

So King Nonn headed south towards the Enchanted Forest, but unfortunately he fell asleep on the way. When he woke up, he said to his horse Palfrey:

"Heavens, I must have dozed off. Now where's this Enchanted Forest? We must have missed it. No wonder, Palfrey—your eyesight's even worse than mine. Come along, we'd better carry on."

King Nonn rode on and said:
"According to the map, there
should be a dragon here. I'd
better leave you at the bottom
of this hill, Palfrey, and climb up to
the top for a better view.
Goodness, it seems to be shaking.

I can smell smoke. It must be a
volcano! Wait there, Palfrey, I'll be
down in a minute."

King Nonn rode on until it was quite dark. As he rode, he talked to his horse Palfrey.

''There's a full moon tonight, but I
don't see any witches.''

King Nonn rode on, and soon it was dawn. He said to his horse Palfrey:

''I just don't understand it. If this map is right, I should be rescuing damsels in distress by now, but I think we're in the Enchanted Forest. Look at all those trees! And I can hear such horrible screams and wailing noises.''

"I must do *something* brave before
we go home, or I'll be out of a job.
But wait a minute, this tree has a
door in it. And there's a key. Perhaps
I'd better open it."

As King Nonn turned the key, the door flew open—and out rushed a ghostly white figure.

"Help! Help!" shrieked King Nonn. Palfrey reared up in fright, and galloped away as fast as his legs would carry him.

"Keep going, palfrey!" cried King
Nonn.

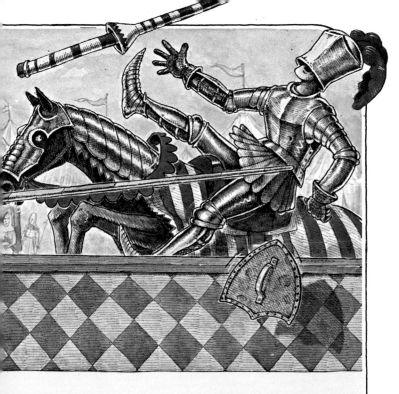

"Oh dear, I seem to have knocked a knight off his horse. Sorry, can't stop!"

Palfrey galloped and galloped, and
King Nonn, hanging on for dear life,
panted:

"Heavens, there are soldiers everywhere. I've knocked some of them over with my lance. Oops, there goes another knight, falling off his horse! What a disaster this adventure has turned out to be!"

A castle loomed up ahead of them, and King Nonn shouted to his horse Palfrey:

''Palfrey, we're home! But whatever's going on? Who are all these people? There are soldiers running in all directions!''

Palfrey pounded over the drawbridge and into the castle.

The Prime Minister was there to greet King Nonn, and took him out on the balcony to wave to his subjects.

"What a triumph, Your Majesty!"
he cried. "What courage! Single-
handed you threw King Blagard of
Rong from his horse, and single-
handed dispersed his army, just as they
were about to attack!"

"B...b...but," stammered King
Nonn.

"Now, don't be modest, the raven
has told us everything," the Prime
Minister went on. "How you braved
a giant and a dragon, fended off a
flock of witches, rode right through
the Enchanted Forest, rescued a
damsel in distress, and even won a
joust with the terrible Black Knight.
Now we have a King to be proud of!"

That night, back in his study, King Nonn told the Prime Minister and the raven what *he* thought had happened, and they told him what *they* thought had happened. They decided to keep the true story a secret. That way, everyone would be happy.

The tales of King Nonn's exploits were told over and over again, each time becoming more heroic and wonderful. He lived to a great age and wrote many books of the art of fighting giants and dragons. And he and Palfrey never had to go on another adventure again.

COLIN McNAUGHTON is one of the leading British illustrators. His first children's book was published in 1976, followed by twenty-five successful picture books, for instance: *The Rat Race, Football Crazy, Miss Brick the Builder's Baby, They Came from Aargh!* Colin is usually the author of his picture books, but he has also illustrated books by Russell Hoban, Allan Ahlberg, as well as the prestigious Andrew Lang's *Pink Fairy Book*.

The only picture books I knew as a child were the comic annuals I was given at Christmas: Beano, Dandy, Topper, Eagle *and* Lion. *Looking back, it's not difficult to see that these comics were the main influence on my work. These, and the films I saw every Saturday morning at my local cinema. Pirate films, knights in armour, cowboys and Indians. Although today I am married, with two wild sons and a lovely French wife, I still like the same things: the escapism of the adventure film and the crazy madness of the comic. I guess I never grew up.*
Colin McNaughton

THE KNIGHT APPRENTICE

Pocket Bears tell you more

A boy growing up to be a knight in the
Middle Ages did not go to school like a boy today.
Instead his parents sent him to live in a nobleman's
house. There he was perhaps taught a little reading,
writing and counting. But his training was mostly
intended to make him brave and tough. He learned
to wrestle, to race and to fight with a sword. He
also learned to ride with one hand only on the reins, leaving
the other free to handle weapons, and to tilt the *quintain*. The
quintain was a swivelling target. The boy had to ride at it in
the exact centre with his lance. If he missed, the quintain
could swing around and hit him on the head. He also had to
look after armour and weapons. There is a picture of a
knight's weapons in King Nonn the Wiser's armoury: the
lance, sword, battle-axe and *mace* (a spiked club). The shields in
the armoury have coats of arms on them. A knight wore a
coat of arms on his ~~ ~~ show who he was.
The knight whom King Nonn the Wiser accidentally
knocked from his horse was wearing a full suit of armour.

JOUSTS AND TOURNAMENTS

The joust was a splendid occasion. It took place on a
rectangular piece of ground, fenced or roped off, and known
as the *lists.* Two knights in armour charged at each other with
their lances from opposite ends of the lists. Each tried to
knock the other from his horse. People came from all around
to see the spectacle and ladies and noblemen watched from
stands like those in the picture. The joust was really a contest
of skill. The knights were supposed to use blunted weapons
to ensure that no one was killed or injured. But before the
joust developed, knights used to take part in much rougher
tournaments. Two bands of knights would charge each other
in a free-for-all, trying to unmount their opponents. Often
men were badly hurt and sometimes killed. Life in the Middle
Ages could be violent. Kings who were happiest reading
books, like King Nonn the Wiser, were unusual!